To Anthony, for always reminding me of
just how loved I am.
To Zoe & James, my two greatest blessings.
To my parents, whose unconditional support
made this book possible.
— **Erika**

To Rachael for walking with me through the fog.
— **Josh**

THE GIVING FARMER
Published by David C Cook
4050 Lee Vance Drive
Colorado Springs, CO 80918 U.S.A.

David C Cook U.K., Kingsway Communications
Eastbourne, East Sussex BN23 6NT, England

The graphic circle C logo is a registered trademark of David C Cook.

LCCN 2018940118
ISBN 978-0-8307-7606-1
eISBN 978-0-8307-7607-8

© 2018 Erika Pizzo
Illustrations © 2018 Josh Lewis

Design by Josh Lewis
Edited by Liz Duckworth and Laura Derico

Text set in Mrs Eaves and Boogaloo

Printed in Shenzhen, Guangdong,
China

1 2 3 4 5 6 7 8 9 10

050118

THE GIVING FARMER

WRITTEN BY Erika Pizzo   **ILLUSTRATED BY** Josh Lewis

"Each one must give as he has decided in his heart,
not reluctantly or under compulsion,
for God loves a cheerful giver."

DAVID **C** COOK
transforming lives together

There once was a farmer, a very faithful farmer.
Every year that went by, he worked harder and harder.

At night he would come home to his wife and say,
"I just work and work and work each day!"

**"Is my work important? I can't figure it out.
It's hard not to have just an ounce of a doubt."**

The very next morning the farmer went to his field.
He saw Sarah the sheep step up to his tractor wheel.

"Hi, Sarah the sheep! Can I help you today?"
the farmer asked, seeing Sarah's dismay.

"My friends and I heard
there's a wolf on the prowl!
We're much too afraid
to go home now!"

The farmer said, with a joyful sound,
"You are welcome to stay here.
You can sleep on our grounds!"

"I don't have much, but what I have I'll give you.
After all, that's what Jesus would do!"

Sarah the sheep slept safe with her friends
while, back at home,
a pack of wolves passed their pen.

The very next morning,
after hearing the word,
Sarah exclaimed,
"You saved me and my herd!"

Sarah the sheep went home with her friends,
and the farmer returned to his work once again.

At night he would come home to his wife and say,
"I just work and work and work each day!"

**"Is my work important?
I can't figure it out.
It's hard not to have
just an ounce of a doubt."**

The very next morning
the farmer went to his field.
He saw Peter the pig
step up to his tractor wheel.

"Hi, Peter the pig. Can I help you today?"
the farmer asked, seeing Peter's dismay.

"We ran out of food on our farm in the country.
If I don't feed my piglets, they will go hungry!"

The farmer said, with a joyful sound,
"Please stay here and eat.
We have lots of food to go 'round!"

**"I don't have much, but what I have I'll give you.
After all, that's what Jesus would do!"**

Peter and the piglets ate corn in his pen,
and the farmcr returned to his work once again.

At night he would come home to his wife and say,
"I just work and work and work each day!"

**"Is my work important?
I can't figure it out.
It's hard not to have
just an ounce of a doubt."**

The very next morning
the farmer went to his field.
He saw Holly the horse
step up to his tractor wheel.

"Hi, Holly the horse. Can I help you today?"
the farmer asked, seeing Holly's dismay.

"There was a great fire. It destroyed all our hay!
We have nowhere to go to eat and to play!"

The farmer said, with a joyful sound,
**"Your friends can play here.
There is hay all around!"**

**"I don't have much, but what I have I'll give you.
After all, that's what Jesus would do!"**

Holly and her friends played and played in the hay,
forgetting the fire that ruined their day.

So Holly the horse went home with her friends,
and the farmer returned to his work once again.

At night he would come home to his wife and say,

"I just work **and work and work** each day!

Is my work important?
I can't figure it out.
It's hard not to have

just an ounce
of a doubt."

His wife said at last,
"Dear, it's time you see what's true!
Let's think about this for a minute or two."

"Because you work so hard for your farm,
Sarah the sheep did not suffer great harm!"

"Danger didn't find her and her friends,
at night when the wolves crept
out of their den."

"Peter the pig had
something to eat,
and his piglets didn't need to
find food on the street!"

"Holly the horse had
a place to play,
and her friends didn't cry
for their field all day!"

Every little part of each and every day,
God is working in His own special way.

If you give with an open heart,
God will be with you right from the start.

The farmer began to smile and smile.
His work *was* important! Each day was worthwhile.

THE END